This book belongs to............................

For Mum and Dad and all those
cherry dip flippers out there

CLEOPATRA SILVERWING
A RED FOX BOOK 0 09 943228 5

First published in Great Britain by The Bodley Head,
an imprint of Random House Children's Books

The Bodley Head edition published 2004
Red Fox edition published 2005

1 3 5 7 9 10 8 6 4 2

Copyright © Adria Meserve, 2004

The right of Adria Meserve to be identified
as the author and illustrator of this work has
been asserted in accordance with the
Copyright, Designs and Patents Act 1988.

Red Fox Books are published
by Random House Children's Books,
61–63 Uxbridge Road, London W5 5SA,
a division of The Random House Group Ltd,
London Sydney Auckland Johannesburg and
agencies throughout the world.

THE RANDOM HOUSE GROUP
Limited Reg. No. 954009
www.kidsatrandomhouse.co.uk

A CIP catalogue record for this book is
available from the British Library.

Printed and bound in Singapore

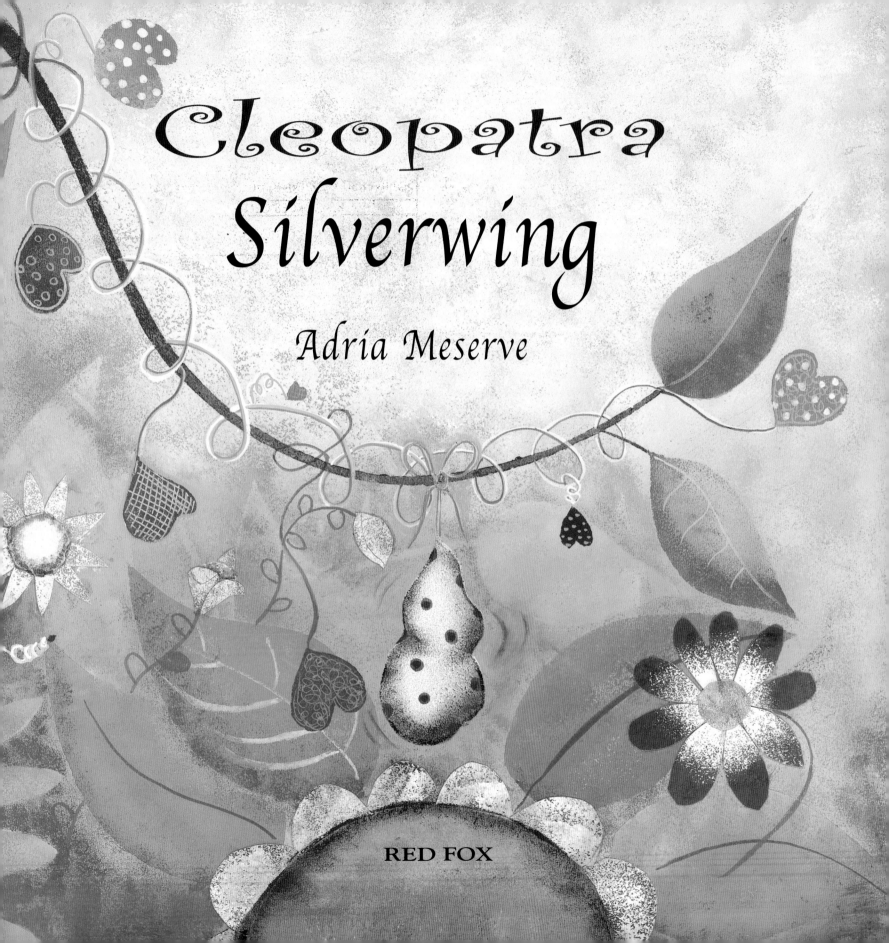

Cleopatra
Silverwing

Adria Meserve

RED FOX

It was the start of spring in the forest. Cleopatra Silverwing squirmed and wriggled out of her chrysalis. She stretched and fluttered her pink and purple reversible wings and began to fly. "Mum! Dad! Look at me!" she called.

While the other
butterflies fluttered
about gently, Cleopatra
learned to do stunts.

She was an expert at loop the loops.

Cleopatra was also the best at
playing hide-and-seek. She knew that
if she hid in a pink and purple flower
no one could ever find her.

. . . 99, 100, 101, 102, 103 . . .

One morning, Cleopatra was dangling high up in a tree, dreaming of adventure.

"Come inside!" her dad called out. *"There's a storm coming!"*

"But I want to practise my cherry dip flip!"
said Cleopatra.

"Don't be silly," said her mum.
"It's far too windy."

Cleopatra sulked.
Then, when she was sure
no one was watching . . .

she tiptoed through the petals . . .

. . . sneaked between the leaves and . . .

. . . spun into a super cherry dip flip.

"Tee, hee! Ha! Ha!"
she giggled as the
wind tickled her
wings.

But then an enormous gust of wind
blew by and and swept Cleopatra away.

It tossed her up over rivers and hills,
higher and higher, until the forest
was a just tiny green dot below.
"What an adventure!"
thought Cleopatra.

It whipped her over snowy mountain peaks
and into thick fluffy clouds. Cleopatra did
so many loop the loops that she became
very dizzy and cold.

"I should fly home," she said.
But she couldn't –
her wings were frozen.

Then suddenly
the wind
dropped her . . .

SPLAT!

into a gooey swamp.

Some grass twitched.

A rock toppled.

Something big zoomed overhead.

A frog opened its hungry mouth and
stuck out its sticky tongue.

Help!
Cleopatra leapt out of the
way just in time. She needed to
hide, but there were no pink and
purple flowers to hide in.
"I want my mum!" she said.

Soon it was dark. Hundreds of scary eyes stared out at Cleopatra. She tucked herself up as small as she could and pretended she was playing a very long game of hide-and-seek.

Suddenly Cleopatra heard a

loud buzzing noise.

She saw a light.

It was coming closer . . .

. . . and closer.

. . . and closer.

It was coming straight for her.

Her heart beat fast.

"Please don't eat me!" she cried.

"I won't eat you," said a firefly, as he landed. "Are you lost?"

Cleopatra trembled. "Mum and Dad told me not to go out in the storm. Now it's dark and I can't find my way home."

"We can light the way," said the firefly. He flashed his glowing bum on and off.

"That's amazing!" said Cleopatra. She didn't know of any bugs in the forest that could do that.

Firefly and his friends lit the way out of the swamp and over the mountains. As the sun came up, Cleopatra could see the forest.

"I can see my flower!"
she said.

She did an extra special loop the loop

and landed on her favourite flower.

Whoopee!

"Thank you," she called as she waved goodbye to the fireflies.

"You're safe!" cried Mr and Mrs Silverwing,
and they gave her a big butterfly kiss.
Her mum and dad and friends had been
looking for her everywhere.

"I promise I won't go off on my own again until I'm much older," said Cleopatra, "and I will always tell you where I am going."

But when the wind
picks up, Cleopatra still loves
showing off her cherry dip flip
to her friends . . .

Wheeeeee!

If you liked my story, you'll love these . . .